Grandma Tell Me A Story

written by
Lynn Floyd Wright

illustrated by
Debbie Pagliughi

WORRYWART PUBLISHING COMPANY
COLUMBIA

To Carol —
Someone extra special —
There are some mighty
lucky children who
you teach!

God bless you!

L Floyd Wright

1995.

Requests should be mailed to:

Worrywart Publishing Company
337 White Birch Circle
Columbia, South Carolina 29223-3228

1 3 5 7 9 10 8 6 4 2

Library of Congress Cataloging-in-Publication Data

Wright, Lynn Floyd, 1957 -
    Grandma, tell me a story / written by Lynn Floyd Wright ; illustrated by Debbie Pagliughi.
       p.   cm.
    Summary: During a bedtime story, grandmothers reassure their grandchildren that even when separated they can remember them by the smell of favorite things.
    ISBN 1-881519-10-4 (alk. paper). -- ISBN 1-881519-11-2 (pbk. : alk. paper)
    (1. Grandmothers – Fiction.   2. Smell – Fiction.   3. Separation anxiety - Fiction.   4. Animals - Fiction.
    5. Bedtime - Fiction.)   I. Pagliughi, Debbie, 1956 - ill.   II. Title.
PZ7. W9565Gr   1999
(E) – dc 21

                                      98-33651
                                         CIP
                                         AC

In memory of Grandma Floyd and Grandmom Van...always in my heart

~LFW~

In loving memory of Betty Pagliughi, who truly lived up to the name "Grandma"

~DP~

Grandmothers...God's perfection in every family

In the dark of night, when all is still, little heads peek out from their beds and plead...

Grandma, tell me a story.

I will tell you a marvelous story about one of my most favorite things. Your neck.

When I hug your neck, I smell all the familiar things around me that I love. So if ever you're far away from me or we can't be together, all I have to do is close my eyes and sniff...

leaves rustling in the wind...

fish washed up on the shore...

strawberries growing in the garden...

wood chopped in the forest...

or grass newly mowed in the field...

and I'll think about you.

And if I take a deep breath and smell...

bananas ripening on a vine...

algae floating atop a pond...

mud thick and gooey after a rain...

honey dripping from a tree...

or hay scattered out in a meadow...

you're with me always. You're as close as my nose!

I love you. Sleep well.

Did you know...

when they are born, **giant pandas** are as small as rats?

an **ostrich** can outrun a horse?

prairie dogs like to sunbathe?

koalas smell just like cough drops because of the kind of eucalyptus (u-cuh-**lip**-tus) leaves they like to eat?

a **mouse** can chirp just like a bird?

a **puffin** can hold as many as eight fish in its beak while swimming?

a **beaver** is so dedicated to its work that anytime it hears the sound of running water-- even if it is coming from inside a house-- it will start building a dam?

all **ponies** are born with a coat of curly hair that becomes straight as it grows up?

a **whale** has a tongue big enough for fifty grown-ups to stand on?

anteaters cannot chew or yawn?

llamas spit when they're angry?

Did you know...

orangutans prefer to live and travel in the treetops and only come down to the ground one or two times a year?

a **flamingo** is born white but turns pink as it gets older because of the food it eats?

when it runs, a **warthog** sticks its tail straight up in the air, like a flag?

because of its heavy fur coat, a **black bear** can eat as much honey as it wants without being stung?

a **pelican** has hollow bones, which keeps it light enough to fly?

ALSO BY LYNN FLOYD WRIGHT

The Prison Bird
Just One Blade
Momma, Tell Me A Story
Flick
Flick The Hero!
Daddy Tell Me A Story

ABOUT THE AUTHOR

LYNN FLOYD WRIGHT has combined two of her favorite things -- family and animals-- in her latest story, *Grandma Tell Me A Story*. A native South Carolinian, she is the author of six other children's books including *The Prison Bird*, *Momma Tell Me A Story*, *Daddy Tell Me A Story* and the very popular Flick dog series, *Flick* and *Flick The Hero!* *Grandma Tell Me A Story* comes from her wonderful memories of childhood visits with her two grandmothers. She and her husband Dave have a large family of their own that includes four children, eight grandchildren, four nieces, a nephew, and two dogs, Skipper and Nellie!

ABOUT THE ILLUSTRATOR

DEBBIE PAGLIUGHI grew up on Long Island, New York. After teaching for three years, she returned to her first loves, drawing and painting, and has combined her favorite subjects of animals and nature in illustrating *Grandma Tell Me A Story*. She and her husband Paul and son David live in the seaside village of Swansboro, North Carolina and share their house with three dogs, a cat, a love bird and a rabbit. This is her third book for children.

ORDER OTHER BOOKS BY LYNN FLOYD WRIGHT

NUMBER	TITLE	PRICE	TOTAL
_____	**THE PRISON BIRD**	$13.95	_____
_____	**FLICK**	$13.95	_____
_____	**MOMMA TELL ME A STORY**	$13.95	_____
_____	**FLICK THE HERO!**	$13.95	_____
_____	**DADDY TELL ME A STORY** (paperback only)	$ 6.95	_____
_____	**GRANDMA TELL ME A STORY** (hardcover)	$13.95	_____
_____	(paperback)	$ 6.95	_____

SUBTOTAL _____

POSTAGE ($1.50 1st book + .50 each add'l.)   + _____

SC Residents only: add 5% sales tax   + _____

TOTAL   _____

☐ Enclosed is my check/money order made payable to: WORRYWART PUBLISHING

SHIP to:

_____

_____

_____

MAIL TO:

WORRYWART PUBLISHING
337 WHITE BIRCH CIRCLE
PO BOX 24911
COLUMBIA, SC 29224-4911